DISCOVERING
CAREERS FOR YOUR FUTURE

performing arts

Ferguson Publishing Company
Chicago, Illinois

Carol Yehling
Editor

Beth Adler, Herman Adler Design Group
Cover design

Carol Yehling
Interior design

Bonnie Needham
Proofreader

Library of Congress Cataloging-in-Publication Data

Discovering careers for your future. Performing arts.
      p. cm.
   Includes index.
   ISBN 0-89434-361-0
    1. Performing arts—Vocational guidance—Juvenile literature. I. Ferguson Publishing Company.

PN1580 .D57 2000
791'.023—dc21

                                     00-037661

Published and distributed by
Ferguson Publishing Company
200 West Jackson Boulevard, 7th Floor
Chicago, Illinois 60606
800-306-9941
www.fergpubco.com

Printed in the United States of America
X-9

Table of Contents

Introduction

You may not have decided yet what you want to be in the future. And you don't have to decide right away. You do know that right now you are interested in one or more of the performing arts. Do any of the statements below describe you? If so, you may want to begin thinking about what a career in the performing arts might mean for you.

___My favorite class in school is music.

___I enjoy performing in front of an audience.

___I take ballet/jazz/tap lessons.

___I take music lessons.

___I try out for parts in school plays.

___I sing in my school or church choir.

___I enjoy putting on plays with my friends.

___I like to make movies with my video camera.

___I listen to music whenever I can.

___I like to write plays.

___I am good at giving speeches and oral presentations.

___I play in the school band or orchestra.

___I see as many movies and plays as I can.

___I enjoy going to live music or dance concerts.

___I like to read biographies of famous performers.

Discovering Careers for Your Future: Performing Arts is a book about careers in the performing arts, from actors to stunt performers. Performing artists include those who work in theater, film, music, and dance. They entertain us, educate us, and help us understand different ways of thinking and feeling.

This book describes many possibilities for future careers in the performing arts. Read through it and see how the different careers are connected. For example, if you are interested in acting, you will want to read the chapters on Actors, Clowns, Comedians, Magicians, Screenwriters, Stage Production Workers, and Stunt Performers. If you are interested in music, you will want to read the chapters on Composers, Music Teachers, Musical Instrument Repairers, Musicians, Pop/Rock Musicians, Singers, and Songwriters. Go ahead and explore!

What do performing artists do?

The first section of each chapter begins with a heading such as "What Actors Do" or "What Dancers Do." It tells what it's like to work at this job. It describes typical responsibilities and assignments. You will find out about working conditions. Which performing artists work in studios? Which ones work in locations all across the country? This section answers all these questions.

How do I become a performing artist?

The section called "Education and Training" tells you what schooling you need for employment in each job—a high school diploma, training at a junior college, a college degree, or more. It also talks about on-the-job training that you could expect to receive after you're hired, and whether or not you must complete an apprenticeship program.

How much do performing artists earn?

The "Earnings" section gives the average salary figures for the job described in the chapter. These figures give you a general idea of how much money people with this job can make. Keep in mind that many people really earn more or less than the amounts given here because actual salaries depend on many different things, such as the size of the company, the location of the company, and the amount of education, training, and experience you have. Generally, but not always, bigger companies located in major cities pay more than smaller ones in smaller cities and towns, and people with more education, training, and experience earn more. Also remember that these figures are current averages. They will probably be different by the time you are ready to enter the workforce.

What will the future be like for performing artists?

The "Outlook" section discusses the employment outlook for the career: whether the total number of people employed in this career will increase or decrease in the coming years and whether jobs in this field will be easy or hard to find. These predictions are based on economic conditions, the size and makeup of the population, foreign competition, and new technology. Terms such as "faster than the average," "about as fast as the average," and "slower than the average," are terms used by the U.S. Department of Labor to describe job growth predicted by government data.

Keep in mind that these predictions are general statements. No one knows for sure what the future will be like. Also remember that the employment outlook is a general statement about an industry and does not necessarily apply to everyone. A determined and talented person may be able to find a job in an industry or career with the worst kind of outlook. And a person without ambition and the proper training will find it difficult to find a job in even a booming industry or career field.

Where can I find more information?

Each chapter includes a sidebar called "For More Info." It lists organizations that you can contact to find out more about the field and careers in the field. You will find names, addresses, phone numbers, and Web sites.

Extras

Every chapter has a few extras. There are photos that show performing artists in action. There are sidebars and notes on ways to explore the field, related jobs, fun facts, profiles of people in the field, or lists of Web sites and books that might be helpful. At the end of the book you will find a glossary and an index. The glossary gives brief definitions of words that relate to education, career training, or employment that you may be unfamiliar with. The index includes all the job titles mentioned in the book. It is followed by a list of general performing arts Web sites.

It's not too soon to think about your future. We hope you discover several possible career choices. Happy hunting!

Actors

Screen Acting and Stage Acting

Screen acting differs from acting in a theater. In screen work, the camera can focus closely on an actor, so performances must be subtle and lifelike. Stage work requires more exaggerated gestures and speaking techniques. Film actors spend a lot of time waiting for scenes to be filmed. They repeat the same scene over and over, play scenes out of order, and perform only small segments of a scene at a time. Stage actors perform an entire play at one time. Screen actors do not know how audiences react to their performance until months after they finish work on a film. Stage actors get an immediate reaction from the audience while they are performing.

What Actors Do

Actors perform in stage plays, movies and television, video, and radio productions. They use voice, movement, and gestures to portray different characters. Actors work many hours before performing in front of an audience. They must first find available parts. They read and study the parts and then audition for the director and producers of the show. In film and television, actors must also do screen tests, which are scenes recorded on film. Once selected for a role, actors memorize their lines and rehearse with other cast members. Rehearsal times are usually longer for live theater performances than for film and television productions. If the production includes singing and dancing, it requires more rehearsal time.

Theater actors may perform the same part many times a week for weeks, months, and sometimes years. Actors in films may spend several weeks on one production,

Indiana University

Actors perform in a production of **The Cherry Orchard** *by Anton Chekov presented by Indiana University Theater.*

which often takes place on location—that is, in different parts of the world. Television actors in a series, such as a soap opera or a situation comedy, also may play the same role for years, generally in 13-week cycles. For these actors, however, their lines change from week to week and even from day to day, and much time is spent rehearsing new lines. Stage actors perform an entire play, beginning to end, in one performance. Television and film actors usually perform scenes out of sequence—they may perform the last scene first, for example. They also may have to repeat the same scene many times.

Acting is often seen as a glamorous profession, yet many actors work long and irregular hours for both rehearsals and

EXPLORING

• Participate in school or community theater productions. You can audition for acting roles, but also work on costumes, props, or lighting to get theater experience.

• See as many plays and movies as you can.

• Read biographies of famous actors and other books about acting, auditioning, theater, and the film and television industries. You can also find biographies of actors on A&E Television Network's Web site at http://www. biography.com.

memory, a fine speaking voice, and, if possible, the ability to sing and dance. Actors who appear in musicals usually have studied singing and dancing for years in addition to their training in drama.

Although it is not required, a college education is helpful. High school and community theaters offer acting opportunities, and large cities such as New York, Chicago, and Los Angeles have public high schools for the performing arts. Special dramatic arts schools, located mainly in New York and Los Angeles, also offer training.

performances, often at low wages. Actors must frequently travel to work in different theaters and on location.

Education and Training

Besides natural talent, actors need determination, a good

Earnings

The wage scale for actors and actresses is set by the unions. Actors in Broadway productions make a minimum weekly salary of $1,235. Those in smaller regional theaters earn from $400 to $600 a week. Nonunion actors often earn much less.

Extras make at least $99 a day for a union performance.

Actors who are members of the Screen Actors Guild earned a daily minimum of $559, or $1,942 a week, in 1997. Because of frequent periods of unemployment, most guild members earned $5,000 or less a year from acting jobs in the 1990s. Unions offer members who meet certain working requirements health, welfare, and pension funds; some even get paid vacation and sick time, depending on their individual contracts.

Outlook

Jobs in acting will grow faster than the average through 2008, but acting is an overcrowded field. In the last two decades, the field has grown considerably outside New York because many major cities have started their own professional theater companies. The number of dinner theaters and summer stock companies has also increased. Cable television programming

FOR MORE INFO

This union represents television and radio performers, including actors, dancers, singers, specialty acts, and stuntpersons.
American Federation of Television and Radio Artists— Screen Actors Guild
260 Madison Avenue
New York, NY 10016
Tel: 212-532-0800

This union represents film and television performers. It has general information on actors, directors, and producers.
Screen Actors Guild
5757 Wilshire Boulevard
Los Angeles, CA 90036-3600
Tel: 213-549-6400

This site has information for beginners on acting and the acting business.
Acting Workshop On-Line
Web: http://www.execpc.com/ ~blankda/acting2.html

continues to add new acting opportunities, but there always will be many more actors than there are roles to play. Many actors also work as secretaries, waiters, taxi drivers, or have other jobs to earn extra income.

Choreographers

What Choreographers Do

Choreographers create original dance routines for dancers to perform. Choreographers have a thorough understanding of dance and music, as well as costume, lighting, and dramatics. Besides inventing new dance routines, choreographers teach their dances to performers and sometimes they direct and stage the presentation of their dances.

Choreographers sometimes specialize in one type of dance, such as ballroom, ballet, modern, jazz, acrobatic, or tap. Others use a variety of styles in one dance routine. Some choreographers create dances for dance companies to perform as part of their repertoire. Others choreograph routines for operas, musical comedies, music videos, movies, and television productions.

Choreographers usually start out as dancers. They study dance for many years and learn all the movements and positions of the various types of dance. Each type of dance has its own movement styles and a vocabulary to describe those movements. Most basic dance movements in American dance come from ballet and use French terms, such as *plié, relevé,* and *arabesque.* Tap dance has steps called flap, shuffle, time-step, and ball-change.

Choreographers know how to use movement and music to tell a story, create a mood, express an idea, or celebrate movement itself. Since dance is so closely related to music, choreographers know about various musical styles and rhythms. They often hear a piece of music first and then choreograph a dance to it. Sometimes choreographers plan the dance, then choose the dancers and teach them movements. But most often they work with their dancers, and change the choreography to take best advantage of the dancers' abilities. Choreographers must also be flexible enough to change their dances to fit different performance spaces.

Education and Training

There are no formal educational requirements, but an early start in dance classes (around eight years old for ballet, slightly older for jazz, tap, modern, folk, or acro-

EXPLORING

• Take as many dance classes as you can. Try different types of dance.

• There are many instructional videos available that teach you ballet, tap, and ballroom dancing. It is best, though, to study with a teacher who can watch you and help you do the movements correctly, so you don't develop bad habits or injure yourself.

• Once you have learned some dance technique, begin to give recitals and performances. Performing and rehearsing will give you experience working with a choreographer.

• Try to choreograph a dance routine for a school performance or community event. Participate in any school or community stage production that has dance numbers.

HOW DO YOU COPYRIGHT CHOREOGRAPHY?

A painting, a novel, a symphony, and other artistic works can be copyrighted to protect them from being stolen and used without the permission of the artists who created them. But how do you copyright choreography? It is difficult to record movements, including gestures and facial expressions, but in order to copyright a dance, there must be some kind of record. These are the methods that can be used to record choreography:

- Video
- Written description
- Drawing stick figures
- Dance notation

Dance notation is the most accurate way to record choreography. The two most common methods are *Labanotation*, named for its inventor, Rudolphe Laban, and *Benesh notation*, created by Rudolphe and Joan Benesh.

Labanotation uses a vertical staff of three lines read from bottom to top. The center line represents the central axis of the body. Weight-bearing movements and leg gestures are indicated by geometrical symbols written inside the staff. Arm, torso, and head movements are written outside the staff. Horizontal marks show musical meter.

Benesh notation uses a horizontal staff, like a musical staff, and is read from left to right. The lines represent the different levels of the body from head to foot. Body movements are written inside the staff and floor patterns are noted below. Rhythm and phrasing are written above the staff.

batic dance) and years of practice are essential. Talented students begin serious training with regional or national dance schools in their early teens. Many dancers have professional auditions by the time they are 17 or 18 years old.

A college degree is not necessarily an advantage for professional choreographers, but there are many colleges that offer degrees in dance with choreography courses.

Earnings

Salaries depend on the size of the theater and earnings from performance royalties and fees. In small professional theaters, choreographers may earn about $1,000 per week, and as much as $30,000 for a Broadway production requiring eight to ten weeks of rehearsal time. When working for big-budget motion pictures, choreographers can earn an average of $3,000 per week. Those working in television can earn up to $10,000 in a 14-day period.

Outlook

Employment for choreographers is expected to grow as fast as the average through the next 10 years, but only the most talented choreographers will find jobs. Very few dancers and choreographers work year round and they often take other jobs to make extra money. More than half the dance companies in the United States are in New York City, which means the majority of choreographers live there, too. There are opportunities in other large cities where there are dance companies and theater companies. There is some work available in film and television, too.

FOR MORE INFO

For information on all aspects of dance, including job listings, send a self-addressed, stamped envelope to:
American Dance Guild
31 West 21st Street, 3rd Floor
New York, NY 10010
Tel: 212-627-3790

A directory of dance companies and related organizations and other information on professional dance is available from:
Dance USA
1156 15th Street, NW, Suite 820
Washington, DC 20005-1704
Tel: 202-833-1717
Web: http://www.danceusa.org

This Web site has extensive listings of library resources, links, and information on various aspects of dance.
Dance Links
Web: http://www.arts.arizona.edu/dance/dancelinks.html

Circus Performers

What Circus Performers Do

Circus performers do daring and dangerous physical acts to entertain and thrill live audiences. *Trapeze artists* leap from one trapeze to another, or do somersaults in midair. *Highwire* or *wire walkers* may walk, ride bicycles, unicycles, or do gymnastic moves on a wire suspended high above the ground. *Acrobats* perform gymnastic routines of many varieties. *Animal trainers* show off the strength or abilities of animals, such as elephants, lions, tigers, and horses, while often appearing to risk their own lives. *Aerialists* perform various athletic feats in the air such as flips and spins. *Jugglers* can keep many objects in the air at once, even if the objects are dangerous ones like fiery rings or knives. *Clowns* perform comedic routines and most circuses also have a circus band whose members keep the action exciting with their musical accompaniment.

Most circuses have several circus performers working at once in different rings. These simultaneous performances are usually introduced by an announcer, known as the *ringmaster,* who calls the audience's attention to one or more rings. Although most circuses at one time were held in outdoor tents, known as big tops, most today are held in large indoor arenas.

Education and Training

Many full-time circus performers were born into circus families. Without coming from a circus family, becoming a circus performer can be difficult. Many acrobats, riders, and other circus performers learn their craft from more experienced performers.

No diploma is required by most circuses. A high school or college education, however, will help you manage your business affairs and communicate with others. Athletic training that develops coordination, strength, and balance is necessary for almost all circus performers. Other training includes acting, music, dance and, for those interested in animals, veterinary care. Knowledge of foreign languages will be helpful for performers who travel overseas.

EXPLORING

• Go to every circus that comes to your area. Talk to the performers about their work.
• Gymnastics teams, drama clubs, and dance troupes give you performance experience and may help you decide if you have talent for this type of work. Physical education classes and community athletic games and competitions provide excellent physical training.
• If you are interested in animal training, volunteer at nearby zoos or stables.
• You may wish to join an association of jugglers, unicyclists, or another specialty. They often hold festivals, events, and seminars where you can learn skills, get to know other circus performers, and perhaps find a mentor who can help you get into the field.

Earnings

According to the Circus World Museum, circus performers just starting out usually do not earn much more than the minimum wage ($5.15 per hour), and sometimes even lower, perhaps $200 to $400 per week. Performers usually receive food and lodging. Less-skilled performers earn $600 to $700 per week, while those who work with animals earn from several thousand per week up to $100,000 or more for the circus season. Performers who develop highly unusual acts and achieve fame or recognition earn the best salaries.

Outlook

Circus performing is not usually permanent full-

CIRCUS SCHOOLS AND CAMPS

Explore these Web sites for information about training in circus arts available across the country.

Adventurous Woman—Circus Sports
Six-week sessions of acrobatics, static trapeze, and trampoline for circus performers and gymnasts in northern California.
http://www.adventurous.com/classes/acrosports/circus99.html

Camp Lohikan's Circus Program
Lake Como, Pennsylvania
Flying trapeze, acrobatics, circus biking, juggling, fire eating, unicycling, clowning, balancing, high wire, spanish web, globe balancing, and more.
http://www.lohikan.com/circus.htm

Cirkids.org
Vancouver, British Columbia
Training for kids ages 5 to 16 in aerials, tightwire, juggling, unicycle, stacking bike, pyramids, tumbling, and much more.
http://www.cirkids.org/

Circus Arts Workshop
McLean, Virginia
http://home.circusarts.com/ectp/

Ecole Nationale de Cirque
Montreal's world renowned circus school where many of Cirque Du Soleil's artists train.
http://www.enc.qc.ca/ta-plan.html

Flying High Circus
Florida State University's circus school and performances—everything from juggling to flying trapeze.
http://mailer.fsu.edu/~mpeters/fsucircus.html

San Francisco School of Circus Arts
Encourages and develops potential, character, and spirit through circus arts.
http://www.sfcircus.org/

time work. The outlook for circus performers does not seem to be improving. Those who work in a resident company of a circus can become well known and have greater job security. There are more opportunities for circus performers outside the circus, and there is always an interest in new, unusual, never-been-seen acts. The private party business is growing, and circus performers may find work in television and music videos.

Circuses have changed in recent years. Fewer circuses use live animals and the trend is toward more theatrical, theme productions. Even with the changes, the popularity of circuses has remained steady and should remain so for the next 10 years. But the number of circus performers is far larger than the number of job openings.

FOR MORE INFO

This organization provides arts and education programs to schools. It also operates Circus Information Referral Center.
Circus Education Specialists
56 Lion Lane
Westbury, NY 11590
Tel: 516-334-2123

This library and research center documents the history of the circus in America. It offers referrals to camps and schools that provide training, as well as to producers and circuses.
Circus World Museum
426 Water Street
Baraboo, WI 53913-2597
Tel: 608-356-8341

This Web site offers facts and information about Ringling, including news, games, animals, history and tradition, performers, and show dates.
Ringling Bros. and Barnum & Bailey
8607 Westwood Center Drive
Vienna, VA 22182
Tel: 608-278-0520
Web: http://www.ringling.com

RELATED JOBS

Actors
Animal Trainers
Clowns
Comedians
Dancers and Choreographers
Magicians
Stunt Performers

Clowns

Clowns Through the Ages

Clowns have been called pranksters, mirthmakers, jesters, comics, jokers, buffoons, harlequins, fools, merry-andrews, mimes, and joeys.

Early Egyptian, Greek, and Roman rulers kept fools for entertainment. During the Middle Ages and the Renaissance, court jesters were hired for their musical and juggling skills and verbal wit. They wore colorful clothing: big collars, bells, pointed caps, and unusual shoes. Many jesters were traveling minstrels, skilled in storytelling, juggling, singing, magic, tightrope walking, and acrobatics.

After the Renaissance, clowns became stage characters, such as country bumpkins or dim-witted servants. The word "clown" was first used in 16th-century England to describe a clumsy, country oaf. Small traveling street theaters used them to attract audiences to their plays.

What Clowns Do

Clowns work in circuses, in movies, on television, in musical plays, at birthday parties and other events, or in fairgrounds or amusement parks. They perform comical routines often while wearing unusual makeup and costumes. They juggle, dance, ride unicycles, walk tightropes, or perform other tricks and skills to make people laugh.

Circus clowns often perform routines to entertain audiences while other acts are being set up. They sing songs, tell jokes, or do acrobatic stunts. Clowns have a good sense of timing and balance and are able to improvise, or make things up on the spot. Every audience is different and clowns change their performances according to how the audience reacts.

The makeup and costumes vary for different kinds of clowns. *Whiteface clowns* wear white makeup and caps that make them appear to be bald. They are the elegant clowns and are often in charge of a routine. *Auguste clowns* wear baggy clothes and act clumsy or silly. They trip over objects on the stage or drop things other clowns are juggling. *Tramp clowns* wear tattered clothes and are sad or forlorn. *Character clowns,* like Charlie Chaplin, have unique routines, and usually perform alone.

Clowns usually have to travel to find work. For jobs with traveling circuses, they travel for much of the year. Circus clowns may perform in a large tent outdoors or in a large indoor arena. Those who work at fairs or amusement parks usually perform outdoors, wandering the grounds, gathering audiences in various locations.

Education and Training

A high school diploma is not required by most circuses, but a diploma and a college education help your job prospects. Employers in the motion-picture and television industry also prefer to hire performers who have diplomas.

Clowns need to move well and use their bodies to communicate with audiences. Training in dance and pantomime is help-

EXPLORING

• Perform in school or community plays.

• Take classes in dance, acting (especially improvisation), mime, or gymnastics. You may find a studio or gym in your area that offers classes in juggling, trampoline, acrobatics, magic, or other skills useful for clowns.

• Volunteer to perform as a clown for hospitals, parades, or charitable events.

• Check your library for books about clowning and clown history. Here are some suggestions: *The Most Excellent Book of How to Be a Clown* by Catherine Perkins (Copper Beech Books, 1996).

Clown Act Omnibus : Everything You Need to Know About Clowning Plus over 200 Clown Stunts by Wes McVicar (Meriwether Publishing, 1987).

Clown Skits for Everyone by Happy Jack Feder (Meriwether Publishing, 1991).

ful. Dance academies and schools for dramatic arts offer classes in pantomime and dance. Many high schools also have drama or dance classes for students.

Clowns should be able to project their voices. Any debate or public speaking clubs can help develop this skill. Clowns need to have good voice control as well as poise before an audience. Participating in school or community plays is good training.

Earnings

There are no set salaries for clowns. Circus clowns earn about $400 to $500 per week. Those who work in nightclubs, casinos, or on Broadway can make as much as $10,000,

CLOWN LINGO

Alley: A circus term for the area that the clowns use for makeup and costume changes. The term, clown alley, now refers to clown groups, clubs, or troupes.

Blow-off: A funny or surprise ending to a clown skit.

Bump a nose: A phrase that means "good luck," similar to saying "break a leg" to an actor about to go on stage.

Double take: Showing surprise or shock at something. The clown looks, looks away, then quickly looks back again.

First of May: A beginner clown. Traditionally a new clown has his or her first performance when the winter weather is over, usually around the first of May (see *plunge*).

Hey Rube: Clowns yell, "Hey Rube," to show they are in some kind of trouble and signal other performers to come to the rescue.

Joey: A clown with at least five years of experience.

Patter: The story or script that goes along with a stunt, , a comic skit, or a ventriloquist's act.

Plunge: The first time a new clown performs in public as a clown (see first of May).

according to the American Guild of Variety Artists. Weekly income can vary widely—clowns may earn $300 one week, $1,000 the next, and nothing the week after that. For a child's birthday party, a clown earns $50 to $500 depending on the length of the party and the performer's popularity.

Outlook

The outlook for people who want to work as clowns is not very promising. There is a tremendous amount of competition, and the field is overcrowded. It can take more than a year to find a job as a clown. Most clowns are not permanently employed and must repeatedly audition for positions. They usually hold other jobs while they search for clowning opportunities. Many clowns volunteer to entertain at hospitals or charitable events. Volunteering is good experience and can lead to paying jobs.

FOR MORE INFO

This labor union is for singers, dancers, variety performers, circus performers, ice skaters, and theme park performers.
American Guild of Variety Artists
184 Fifth Avenue
New York, NY 10019

This organization provides arts and education programs to schools. It also operates Circus Information Referral Center.
Circus Education Specialists
56 Lion Lane
Westbury, NY 11590
Tel: 516-334-2123

For information on clown alleys, an annual convention, and competitions, contact:
Clowns of America International
PO Box 6468
Lee's Summit, MO 64064
Tel: 888-52CLOWN
Web: http://www.clown.org

RELATED JOBS

Actors
Circus Performers
Comedians
Magicians
Stunt Performers

Comedians

Joke Search

These Web sites have lots of jokes to get you started. Practice telling them to friends and classmates. Which jokes get the most laughs?

KidsJokes.com
http://www.kidsjokes.com

Laugh-Lines
http://www.laugh-lines.com/kids.shtml

Scatty.com
http://www.scatty.com

Wicked4Kids
http://www.wicked4kids.com

No Kids Allowed
http://www.nokidsallowed.com/jokes

What Comedians Do

Comedians try to make people laugh. Some entertain audiences in nightclubs and at concerts. Some perform in comedy shows on television. Some work behind the scenes writing jokes, sketches, and screenplays for other comedians and actors.

Comedians who perform alone on stage are called *stand-up comedians.* They entertain audiences with stories, jokes, one-liners, and impressions. In comedy clubs in large cities, comedians may do more than one show a night. Each performance can last anywhere from 10 minutes to an hour.

Stand-up comedians travel from city to city entertaining different types of audiences. They change their routines to appeal to different groups of people. To arrange out-of-town performances, comedians may call the club owners themselves or hire a booking agent. In medium- and small-sized cities comedians may give only one performance and then drive or fly to the next city. Stand-up comedians also entertain at conventions, concerts, hotels, parties, and outdoor festivals.

Some comedians perform as members of an improvisational group, such as Chicago's Second City, NBC's *Saturday Night Live,* or ABC's *Whose Line Is It Anyway?* They perform skits, dances, and musical numbers, often making up their own dialogue on the spot.

Only the best comedians appear on television or in movies. They have worked for many years developing their routines and sharpening their skills. Their popularity is the result of hard work, performing experience, and persistence. Comedians often speak of "paying their dues," which means working in not-so-desirable clubs for unappreciative, critical audiences and for low pay.

Education and Training

There is no way to become a comedian except to step on a stage and perform. It takes a great deal of work and practice to become a good comedian. It takes many hours on stage to know how to deliver a

EXPLORING

• Many improvisational groups offer classes in acting and performance techniques. These groups are often highly competitive, but they are a good place to learn skills, make contacts, and have fun.
• Before you get on stage to perform for strangers, try performing for family and friends.
• Most comedy clubs and coffee houses have open mike nights where aspiring comedians can get on stage and try out their material in front of a live audience.
• Acting in school plays and local productions is a good way to get experience.
• Learn by watching. Go to a comedy club or coffee house to observe comedians. Watch comedy performances on television or rent videos that feature live stand-up comedians.

joke, plan the pace of a show, and figure out on the spot what will make a particular audience laugh.

There are no specific education requirements for comedians, but certain school subjects can be helpful. English and composition will help you write jokes well. Speech and drama classes will help develop your performing skills.

Earnings

Stand-up comedians do not earn regular salaries. They are paid either per show or for a week of performances. Comedians who are starting out may earn as little as $20 for a 20-minute show. Those who perform at colleges earn about $500 per show. Comedians who open a show for the main attraction can earn from $125 to $350 per week.

A headline comedian in a comedy club in a large city can earn from $1,000 to $20,000. In

STAND-UP TO TV STARDOM

Early comedians Milton Berle, George Burns and Gracie Allen, Jack Benny, Jackie Gleason, and Lucille Ball all starred in their own television shows. Here are some modern TV stars who started as stand-up comedians:

Bill Cosby, *The Cosby Show*
Ellen DeGeneres, *Ellen*
Jerry Seinfeld, *Seinfeld*
Drew Carey, *The Drew Carey Show, Whose Line Is It Anyway?*
Tim Allen, *Home Improvement*
Jeff Foxworthy, *The Jeff Foxworthy Show*
David Letterman, *The Late Show*
Jay Leno, *The Tonight Show*
Tracey Ullman, *Tracey Takes On*
Gary Shandling, *The Larry Sanders Show*
Rosie O'Donnell, *The Rosie O'Donnell Show*
Steve Harvey, *The Steve Harvey Show*

smaller clubs, headline comedians make between $300 to $800 per show. Those who are just starting out earn very little but can make valuable contacts with club owners, agents, and other comedians. The comedy club usually pays for the comedian's lodging.

Those who write jokes for famous comedians usually get paid around $50 for every joke used. The writers for a network comedy show can earn anywhere from $50,000 to $150,000 or more a year.

FOR MORE INFO

Contact the following organizations for more information on professional comedy careers.

The Association of Comedy Artists
PO Box 1796
New York, NY 10025
Tel: 212-864-6620

National Comedians Association
581 Ninth Avenue, Suite 3C
New York, NY 10036
Tel: 212-875-7705

Off the Cuff

These Web sites have information on improvisational theater and descriptions of improv games you can play with your fellow actors and comedians.

The Improv Page
http://www.ece.uwaterloo.ca/
~broehl/improv/index.html

The Living Playbook
http://www.ece.uwaterloo.ca
/~broehl/improv/index.html

Hugh's List of Improv Handles
http://www.staircase.org/structures/

Fuzzy's Games List
http://www.lowrent.net/super/
improv/games.html

Outlook

There are hundreds of comedy clubs across the country (usually in larger cities) and each club needs performers to get their audiences laughing. The spread of legalized gambling across the United States and the opening of many resorts and theme parks continue to add new opportunities for comedians. Thousands of comedians will continue to find work into the next decade.

Composers

Words to Learn

Composers use these words to tell musicians how loud or soft to play:

pianissimo (pp): very soft

piano (p): soft

mezzopiano (mp): half soft

diminuendo or *descrescendo (dim; decresc. or >):* growing softer

mezzoforte (mf): half loud

forte (f): loud

fortissimo (ff): very loud

crescendo (cres. or <): growing louder

fortepiano (fp): loud, then soft

sforzando or *sforzato (sf; sfz):* sudden, strong accent

Composers use these words to tell musicians how fast or slow to play:

largo: slow and noble

adagio: not as slow as largo

lento: slow; between adagio and andante

andante: moderately slow

moderato: moderate

allegretto: moderately fast

allegro: fast

vivace: lively

presto: very fast

What Composers Do

Composers write music for musical stage shows, television commercials, movies, ballet and opera companies, orchestras, pop and rock bands, jazz combos, and other musical performing groups. Composers work in many different ways. Often they begin with a musical idea and write it down using standard music notation. They use their music training and their own personal sense of melody, harmony, rhythm, and structure. Some compose music as they play an instrument and may or may not write it down.

Most composers specialize in one style of music, such as classical, jazz, country, rock, or blues. Some combine several styles. Composers who work on commission or on assignment meet with their clients to discuss the composition's theme, length, style, and the number and types of performers. Composers work at home, in offices, or in music studios. Some need to work alone to plan and

A composer uses an electronic keyboard and computer software to write a new piece of music.

IBM

build their musical ideas and others work with fellow musicians. Composing can take many long hours of work, and composing jobs may be irregular and low-paying. However, it is extremely satisfying for composers to hear their music performed, and successful commercial music composers can earn a lot of money. After the piece is completed, the composer usually attends rehearsals and works with the performers. The composer may have to revise parts of the piece until the client and the composer are satisfied.

Many composers never perform their own works, but others, especially pop, rock, jazz, country, or blues performers, compose music for their own bands to play.

EXPLORING

• Participate in musical programs offered by local schools, YMCA/YWCAs, and community centers.
• Learn to play a musical instrument, such as the piano, guitar, violin, or cello.
• Attend concerts and recitals.
• Read about music and musicians and their careers.
• Form or join a musical group and try to write music for your group to perform.

Education and Training

All composers need to have a good ear and be able to notate, or write down, their music. Composers of musicals, symphonies, and other large works must have years of study in a college, conservatory, or other school of music. Composers of popular songs may not need as much training. However, studying music helps you develop and express your musical ideas better. Music school courses for those who wish to be composers include music theory, musical form, music history, composition, conducting, and arranging. Composers also play at least one musical instrument, usually piano, and some play several instruments.

Earnings

Most composers earn very little and work only part-time, while a few earn a great deal. Some

PROFILE: WOLFGANG AMADEUS MOZART

Mozart (1756-91) was one the outstanding masters of the Classical Period. He composed works in almost every form and his masterpieces are standard repertoire for piano, symphony orchestra, and opera.

Mozart began his musical studies with his father, Leopold, when he was four years old. He played the clavichord and harpsichord, and composed minuets and other pieces. At the age of six, with his sister Marianne, Mozart gave concerts in Munich and Vienna. He wrote his first opera, La finta semplice, in 1768. At the age of 13, he became director of concerts for the archbishop of Salzburg.

Mozart died at the age of 35 from illness and overwork, and was buried in an unmarked pauper's grave. During his short lifetime, he composed more than 600 works, including more than 25 piano concertos, more than 40 symphonies, and numerous string quartets, piano sonatas, operas, divertimenti, serenades, and dance music.

composers work on commission. When a piece of music is commissioned, the composer receives a lump sum for writing it. Other composers work under contract with a music publishing or recording company. Their compositions become the property of the company. Some composers receive royalties, or payments for each performance or sale of the piece.

For music written for the theater, pay is based on the size and type of the theater company or play. Composers for the theater earn from $3,000 to $12,000 per show. A small opera company may pay in the range of $10,000 to $70,000. Large opera companies pay from $15,000 to $150,000.

A film for a major studio may pay a composer $50,000 to $200,000 or more for a musical score. A composer may be paid per episode for a television program or series, ranging from $1,000 to $8,000.

FOR MORE INFO

Contact the following organizations for information on career opportunities for composers.

American Composers Alliance
170 West 74th Street
New York, NY 10023
Tel: 212-362-8900

American Federation of Musicians of the United States and Canada
1501 Broadway, Suite 600
New York, NY 10036
Tel: 212-869-1330
Web: http://www.afm.org

American Society of Composers, Authors, and Publishers
One Lincoln Plaza
New York, NY 10023
Web: http://www.ascap.com

Outlook

As long as there are commercials, movies, musicals, operas, and orchestras, and other musical performers, there will be a need for composers to write music. Employment should have average growth through 2008.

Dancers

What Dancers Do

Dancers use body movements to tell a story, express an idea or feeling, or entertain their audiences. Professional dancers often belong to a dance company, a group of dancers that work together on a repertoire, a collection of dances they perform regularly.

Most dancers study some ballet or classical dance. *Classical dance* training gives dancers a good foundation for most other types of dance. Many of the standard dance terms used in all types of dance are the same terms used in 17th-century ballet. Traditionally, ballet dance told stories, although today's ballets express a variety of themes and ideas.

Modern dance developed early in the 20th century as a departure from classical ballet. Early modern dancers danced barefoot and began to explore movement and physical expression in new ways. *Jazz dance* is a form of modern dance

Carnegie-Mellon University

Ballet dancers spend many hours in the studio training their bodies and practicing dance routines.

often seen in Broadway productions. *Tap dance* combines sound and movement as dancers tap out rhythms with metal cleats attached to the toes and heels of their shoes. Other dance forms include ballroom dance, folk or ethnic dance, and acrobatic dance.

Dancers may perform in classical ballets, musical stage shows, folk dance shows, television shows, films, and music videos. Because dancing jobs are not always available, many dancers work as part-time dance instructors. Dancers who create new ballets or dance routines are called *choreographers.* (See *Choreographers.*)

Dancers begin training early and have fairly short careers. Most professional ballet and modern dancers retire by age 40 because of the physical demands on their

EXPLORING

• Take as many dance classes as you can. Try different types of dance.
• There are many instructional videos available that teach you ballet, tap, and ballroom dancing. It is best, though, to study with a teacher who can watch you and help you do the movements correctly, so you don't develop bad habits or injure yourself.
• Once you have learned some dance technique, begin to give recitals and performances.
• Audition for school or community stage productions that have dance numbers.

bodies. They become dance teachers, artistic directors, choreographers, or they start other careers.

Education and Training

Dancers usually begin training around the age of 10, or even as early as age seven or eight.

They may study with private teachers or in ballet schools. Dancers who show promise in their early teens may receive professional training in a regional ballet school or a major ballet company. By the age of 17 or 18, dancers begin to audition for positions in professional dance companies.

Many colleges and universities offer degrees in dance. Although a college degree is not required for dancers, it can be helpful. Those who teach dance in a college or university often are required to have a degree. Also, since the professional life of a dancer can be rather short, a college degree can give a dancer better options for a second career after retiring from dance performance.

Earnings

The minimum weekly salary for dancers in ballets and other stage productions is between $610 and $1,275. Most dance contracts last from 36 to 45 weeks.

Modern dance companies usually pay a base salary of $500 to $1,200 per week for a 42- to 44-week season. In smaller companies, pay is about $50 per performance and $5 per hour of rehearsal time. The single performance rate for new first-year ballet dancers is $230. Dancers on tour are paid extra for room and board expenses. Minimum performance rates for dancers on television average $569 for a one-hour show, which generally includes 18 hours of rehearsal time.

Outlook

Job opportunities for dancers will have average growth through 2008. However, there will still be more dancers seeking jobs than there are openings. Local ballet companies will offer the most job opportunities.

FOR MORE INFO

For information on all aspects of dance, including job listings, send a self-addressed, stamped envelope to:
American Dance Guild
31 West 21st Street, 3rd Floor
New York, NY 10010
Tel: 212-627-3790

A directory of dance companies, related organizations, and other information on professional dance is available from:
Dance USA
1156 15th Street, NW, Suite 820
Washington, DC 20005-1704
Tel: 202-833-1717
Web: http://www.danceusa.org

Information on purchasing directories about colleges and universities that teach dance is available from:
National Dance Association
1900 Association Drive
Reston, VA 22091
Tel: 800-321-0789
Web: http://www.aahperd.org/nda/nda-main.html

This Web site has listings of library resources, links, and information on various aspects of dance.
Dance Links
Web: http://www.arts.arizona.edu/dance/dancelinks.html

Disc Jockeys

RELATED JOBS

Actors
Broadcast Engineers
Comedians
Newscasters, Reporters, and Announcers
Radio and Television Program Directors
Radio Producers
Reporters

What Disc Jockeys Do

Disc jockeys, or *DJs,* play recorded music on radio or during parties, dances, and special occasions. On the radio they also announce the time, the weather forecast, and important news. Sometimes DJs interview guests, take calls from listeners, and make public service announcements.

Unlike radio and television newscasters, disc jockeys most often do not have to read from a written script, except for scripted commercials. Their comments are usually spontaneous. Most radio shows are live broadcasts, and since anything may happen while DJs are on the air, they must react calmly under stress and know how to handle unexpected events. The best disc jockeys have pleasant, soothing voices and a talent for keeping listeners entertained.

Disc jockeys often work irregular hours, and most work alone. Some have to report for work at a very early hour in the

A disc jockey announces the next recording he will play on his radio show.

morning or late into the night, because so many radio stations broadcast 24 hours a day. Work in radio stations is demanding. Every activity or comment on the air must begin and end exactly on time. This can be difficult, especially when the disc jockey has to handle news, commercials, music, weather, and guests within a certain time frame. It takes a lot of skill to work the controls, watch the clock, select music, talk with someone, read reports, and entertain the audience. Usually several of these tasks must be performed at the same time.

Disc jockeys must always be aware of pleasing their audiences. They play the

EXPLORING

• Participate in debate or speech clubs to work on your speaking skills and your ability to think and react quickly.

• Try to get a summer job at a radio station.

• Take advantage of any opportunity you get to speak or perform before an audience. Try any type of announcing, such as at sports events.

• Offer to be the DJ at friends' parties or school dances.

THE FIRST DJ

The first major contemporary disc jockey in the United States was Alan Freed (1921-65), who worked in the 1950s on WINS radio in New York. In 1957, his rock and roll stage shows at the Paramount Theater made front-page news in the *New York Times* because of the huge crowds they attracted. The title "disc jockey" started because most music was recorded on conventional flat records or discs.

music their listeners like and talk about the things their listeners want to talk about. If listeners begin to switch stations, ratings go down, and disc jockeys can lose their jobs. DJs who become popular with their audiences and stay with a station for a long time sometimes become famous local personalities.

Education and Training

There is no formal education required for disc jockeys. Many large stations prefer to hire people who have had some college education. Some schools train students for broadcasting, but such training will not necessarily improve the chances of finding a job at a radio station. When hiring DJs, station managers consider an applicant's personality and listen carefully to audition tapes.

If you want to become a disc jockey and possibly advance to other broadcasting positions, attend a college or technical school that has broadcasting or announcing programs. Working at a college radio station can give you valuable experience. Many DJs start out at small radio stations operating equipment and taping interviews.

Earnings

Disc jockeys can earn anywhere from $7,100 to over $100,000 a year. The average salary is $31,251 a year. Those who work for small stations earn the lowest salaries. Top personalities in large market stations earn the most.

Outlook

In the broadcasting field there are usually more job applicants than job openings. As a result, competition is stiff. Beginning jobs in small radio stations usually are easiest to find.

According to the *Occupational Outlook Handbook,* employment of announcers is expected to decline slightly through 2008. Due to this decline, competition will be great in an already competitive field.

Small stations will still hire beginners, but on-air experience will be increasingly important.

FOR MORE INFO

For more information, contact the following organizations:
Broadcast Education Association
1771 N Street, NW
Washington, DC 20036-2891
Tel: 202-429-5354
Web: http://www.beaweb.org

National Association of Broadcasters
1771 N Street, NW
Washington, DC 20036-2891
Tel: 202-429-5300
Web: http://www.nab.org

Radio-Television News Directors Association
1000 Connecticut Avenue, NW, Suite 615
Washington, DC 20036-5302
Tel: 202-659-6510
Web: http://www.rtnda.org

You may have an advantage over other job applicants if you know a lot about a specific area such as business, political, or health news, or if you have an extensive knowledge of a particular kind of music.

Film and Television Directors

What Film and Television Directors Do

Film and television directors coordinate the making of a film. They work with actors, costume designers, camera operators, lighting designers, and producers. Directors are involved in every stage from hiring actors to editing the final film.

Producers are in charge of the business and financial side of a television or film project. *Directors* are in charge of the creative and technical side. Usually a producer hires the director, but they work closely together. They plan a budget and production schedule, including time for research, filming, and editing.

Directors work with the scriptwriter, actors, studio technicians, and set designers. They give directions to many different people. They choose costumes, scenery, and music. During rehearsals they plan the action carefully, telling actors how to move and interpret the script. They coach the actors to help them give their best performances. At the same time, directors give directions for sets and lighting, and decide on the order and angles of camera shots. Once filming is finished, they supervise film editing and add sound and special effects.

Film and television directors work on television commercials, documentaries, music videos, television shows and movies, feature films, industrial films, and travelogues. Most directors specialize in one type of film. Some television directors work on regular shows or series, such as soap operas, situation comedies, sporting events, talk shows, and game shows. These directors work at a console with a row of television monitors. The monitors show what is going on in different parts of the studio from different camera angles.

Education and Training

You can start now to prepare for a career in film directing. Take English literature classes to learn storytelling techniques. Theater classes teach you about acting. Photography courses can teach you about visual composition.

EXPLORING

• Watch movies every chance you get, both at the theater and at home. Study your favorite television shows to see what makes them interesting.

• Two major trade publications to read are *Daily Variety* and *Hollywood Reporter*.

• Many camps and workshops offer programs for students interested in film work. For example, the University of Wisconsin offers its Summer Art Studio for students in grades 7 through 12. In addition to film courses, there are classes in drawing, painting, photography, and television and video. For information, write to the University of Wisconsin-Green Bay, Office of Outreach, TH 335, Green Bay, WI 54311.

Even though there are no specific requirements for becoming a movie or television director, the most successful ones have a wide variety of talents and experience, as well as good business and management skills. You must be able to develop ideas, and be good at communicating with others.

There are many colleges and universities that offer film majors with concentration in directing. These programs require you to direct your own films. They also offer internship and other practical learning experiences. George Lucas's first film, *THX 1138,* was adapted from a short film he made as a student at the University of Southern California film school. The Directors Guild of America offers an Assistant Directors Training Program for those who have a bachelor's degree or two years of experience in movie or television production. (See *For More Info.*)

Many directors begin at small television stations or community the-

THE BEST DIRECTORS

The Academy of Motion Picture Arts and Sciences awarded Oscars to these directors:

1999 Sam Mendes, *American Beauty*
1998 Steven Spielberg, *Saving Private Ryan*
1997 James Cameron, *Titanic*
1996 Anthony Minghella, *The English Patient*
1995 Mel Gibson, *Braveheart*

The Academy of Television Arts and Sciences awarded Emmys to these directors for the 1998-1999 television season:

Outstanding Directing for a Comedy Series: Thomas Schlamme, *Sports Night*, Pilot

Outstanding Directing for a Drama Series: Paris Barclay, *NYPD Blue*, "Hearts And Souls"

Outstanding Directing for a Variety or Music Program: Paul Miller, *1998 Tony Awards*

Outstanding Directing for a Miniseries or a Movie: Allan Arkush, *The Temptations*

aters, or as production assistants for films. Many directors have worked for a number of years as actors, or in some other capacity within the industry, to gain experience.

Earnings

Salaries are arranged by the producer of a film and the Directors Guild of America, which sets fees in the industry. However, well-known directors can arrange for salaries that are higher than average. Salaries vary greatly in this field. Directors of television shows are paid by the type of show. For example, directors of soap operas can earn $2,000 per episode. Movie directors average from $5,100 to $8,000 per week, depending on the total budget for the film. Film directors often negotiate to receive a percentage of the film's profits in addition to their weekly salaries.

FOR MORE INFO

For information about the Assistant Directors Training Program, contact:
Directors Guild—Assistant Directors Training Program
15503 Ventura Boulevard
Encino, CA 91436-3140
Tel: 818-386-2545
Web: http://www.dga.org

For a list of film schools and for articles about the film industry, visit the AFI Web site:
American Film Institute
2021 North Western Avenue
Los Angeles, CA 90027
Tel: 323-856-7600
Web: http://afionline.org

Outlook

Because of an increase in the cable television and video-rental industries, the employment outlook for movie and television directors is good. Employment should grow faster than average through 2008. However, many people are interested in becoming directors and there will be stiff competition for jobs.

Magicians

Famous Magicians

Performers, such as the Sicilian Count Alessandro di Cagliostro (1743-95), the Frenchman Robert-Houdin (1805-71), and the American Harry Houdini (1874-1926), captured the imaginations of audiences with their skill, training, and imagination.

In recent times, magic has lost some of its mystery and become accepted as a performance art. Today, well-known magicians, such as David Copperfield and Lance Burton, entertain people all over the world. More controversial are the popular and less-traditional duo Penn & Teller, who sometimes reveal the secrets of their illusions.

What Magicians Do

Magicians are masters of illusion. They use a combination of complicated moves and persuasive comments to make audiences believe they can pull a rabbit out of a hat, make objects appear and disappear, and make people float in mid-air.

Magicians use tricks and a variety of props, such as illusion boxes, cards, or coins. They often use volunteers from the audience. For example, they might secretly remove a volunteer's watch and make it reappear in someone else's pocket. Or, a magician may use a wooden box or other prop to appear to cut a trained assistant in half with a saw. Each magician has a unique style and many specialize in one type of magic, such as card tricks, or escape art.

There are two basic elements to a magician's performance. The first element is the technique, the actual mechanics of performing illusions or tricks. Magicians practice each movement many times until they can do the trick perfectly. The magician's presentation of an illusion is the second element. The illusions must be exciting and entertaining to keep the audience's attention. Magicians are masters at directing an audience's attention to certain areas and away from others with flashy movements and verbal distractions.

Magicians usually work indoors in front of audiences. They may perform in front of large crowds at a theater or for just a few people at a birthday party. They often work alone, but they sometimes use one or two assistants.

Education and Training

Magicians are skilled entertainers. It can take years of practice to become an accomplished magician, but it is often possible to learn some basic tricks in just a short time.

Professional magicians rarely tell how they perform their tricks. Because of this code of silence, the most common form of training is for a budding magician to study with a professional magician. Many beginning magicians start their careers as assistants for more experienced magicians.

EXPLORING

• You can begin to learn magic tricks on your own. Ask your librarian to help you find books that explain how to do simple tricks.

• Visit a magic shop to explore the different kinds of props and tools magicians use. Magic shops may also have bulletin boards with postings of club meetings or workshops in your area.

• Once you learn a few tricks, begin to perform for your family and friends.

People generally do not take college or high school courses to learn magic tricks, although courses in acting or public speaking can improve your performance skills. You also need to learn good business skills, as magicians usually must handle their own financial matters.

port themselves financially. They often perform nights or on weekends and have other full- or part-time jobs. A magician may earn anywhere from $50 for performing at a birthday party to several thousand dollars for performing at a business meeting or magic show. Many

Earnings

While world-famous magicians, such as David Copperfield, can earn many thousands of dollars for each performance, most magicians do not earn enough from their performances to sup-

Say the Magic Word

Legerdemain
Prestidigitation
Sleight of hand

All of these terms have to do with the expression, "The hand is quicker than the eye." But just as often, magicians rely on a psychological or verbal maneuver to distract you from their manual trickery.

MORE THAN ONE KIND OF MAGIC

Historically, there is white magic and black magic. White magic is beneficial. It cures sickness, makes crops grow, and ensures success in all lines of endeavor. Black magic, or sorcery, causes sickness, accidents, and death; the spoiling of crops; and drought, flood, and other misfortunes. Often the difference between black magic and white is the point of view. A shaman makes white magic to ensure his tribe's victory in battle, but his work is black magic to the enemy, whose warriors are killed and whose villages are raided.

magicians remain amateurs, and some practicing magicians view magic and performing as a hobby, rather than as a career. According to the Society of American Magicians, those who work part-time earn as much as $15,000 to $20,000 a year, while full-time professionals may earn as much as $60,000 to $120,000 a year.

Outlook

The employment outlook for magicians is insecure. Highly skilled magicians should find many job opportunities, while those just starting out in the field may find it difficult to find work. To be successful, magicians must spend a lot of time promoting themselves and hunting for jobs at parties, special events, business meetings, schools, fairs, amusement parks, and conventions.

FOR MORE INFO

For information on workshops and seminars, contact:

International Brotherhood of Magicians
11155 South Towne Square, Suite C
St. Louis, MO 63123
Tel: 314-845-9200
Email: no1inmagic@aol.com
Web: http://www.magician.org

Society of American Magicians
PO Box 510260
St. Louis, MO 63151
Tel: 314-846-5659
Email: rmblowers@aol.com
Web: http://www.magicsam.com/

RELATED JOBS

Actors
Circus Performers
Clowns
Comedians
Singers
Special Effects Technicians
Stage Production Workers
Stunt Performers

Music Teachers

Music Teachers in the Movies

If you have ever taken music lessons, you know how music teachers can affect you. Sometimes you hate them, sometimes you love them. But if you study with one teacher for a long time, you find that they have a great influence on your life, whether you become a musician or not. These movies explore the theme of relationships between music teachers and their students.

Svengali (1931)
starring John Barrymore

It's Great to Be Young (1956)
starring John Mills

Madame Sousatzka (1988)
starring Shirley MacLaine

Mr. Holland's Opus (1995)
starring Richard Dreyfuss

Music of the Heart (1999)
starring Meryl Streep

What Music Teachers Do

Music teachers teach people how to sing, play musical instruments, and appreciate and enjoy the world of music. They teach private lessons and classes. They may work at home or in a studio, school, college, or conservatory. Many music teachers are also performing musicians.

Teachers help students learn to read music, develop their voices, breathe correctly, and hold and play their instruments properly. As their students master the techniques of their art, teachers guide them through more and more difficult pieces of music. Music teachers often organize recitals or concerts that feature their students. These recitals allow family and friends to hear how well the students are progressing and helps students get performing experience.

Private music teachers may teach children who are just beginning to play or sing, teens who hope to make music their

A music teacher teaches a variety of vocal techniques to a large choir.

career, or adults who are interested in music lessons for their own enjoyment.

Music teachers in elementary and secondary schools often offer group and private lessons. They direct in-school glee clubs, concert choirs, marching bands, or orchestras. College and university teachers are also frequently performers or composers. They divide their time between group and individual instruction and may teach several music subjects, such as music appreciation, music history, theory, and pedagogy (the teaching of music).

Education and Training

If you are interested in becoming a music teacher, you probably are already taking

EXPLORING

• Sing in your school or church choir. Join a band or orchestra. Get as much experience as you can playing, singing, and performing.
• Read all you can about music theory, music history, famous musicians, and performance.
• Talk to your music teachers about what they like and don't like about teaching music. Ask them how they became music teachers.

METHODS FOR TEACHING MUSIC

There are several well known methods for teaching music to young children.

1. The **Suzuki** method of music education was begun in the mid-1900s by Japanese violinist Shinichi Suzuki (1898-1998). He believed that the best way to learn music is to be exposed to it from a very early age. He thought young children should learn to play an instrument in the same way that they learn to speak and read—by listening, absorbing, and copying.

In the beginning, the parent is given the first lessons on the instrument, while the child watches. In this way, the child becomes interested in copying the parent. When the child begins learning, it is by ear. Music reading is taught later, at abut the same age a child learns to read books.

2. The **Orff-Schulwerk** system for teaching music to children was started by Carl Orff (1895-1982). It is based on rhythmic and verbal patterns and the pentatonic scale. Orff believed that music was connected with movement, dance, and speech.

Orff-Schulwerk uses poems, rhymes, games, songs, and dances as examples and basic materials. Improvisation and composition are key to learning and appreciating music.

3. The **Kodaly** philosophy is based on the work of Zoltan Kodaly (1882-1967). He believed it was important for children to sing, play instruments, and dance from memory. Children start learning traditional songs, games, chants, and folk songs and later learn music of other cultures and countries. The Kodaly method also involves performing, listening to, and analyzing the great art music of the world, as well as mastering musical skills, such as reading and writing music, singing, and part-singing.

voice lessons or are learning to play an instrument. Participation in music classes, choral groups, bands, and orchestras is also good preparation for a music teaching career.

Like all musicians, music teachers spend years mastering their instruments or developing their voices. Private teachers need no formal training or licenses, but most have spent years studying with an experienced musician, either in a school or conservatory or through private lessons.

Teachers in elementary schools and high schools must have a state-issued teaching license. There are about 600 conservatories, universities, and colleges that offer bachelor's degrees in music education to qualify students for state certificates.

To teach music in colleges and schools of music or in conservatories, you must usually have a graduate degree in music. However, very talented and well-known performers or composers are sometimes hired without any formal graduate training. Only a few people reach that level of fame.

FOR MORE INFO

For more information about a career as a music teacher, contact:
Music Educators National Conference
1806 Robert Fulton Drive
Reston, VA 22091
Web: http://www.menc.org/index2.html

Music Teachers National Association
Carew Tower
441 Vine Street, Suite 505
Cincinnati, OH 45202-2814
Web: http://www.mtna.org

Earnings

Salaries for music teachers vary depending on the type of teaching, the number of hours spent teaching, and the skill of the teacher. Private teachers who instruct beginning and intermediate students charge from $10 to $50 an hour. Public elementary school teachers earn average salaries of $37,000 a year. Public secondary school teachers earn about $39,100 a year.

average rate in elementary schools and colleges and universities, but at a slower rate in secondary schools. When schools face budget problems, music and other art programs are often the first to be cut. Competition has also increased as more instrumental musicians enter teaching because of the lack of performing jobs.

Outlook

Opportunities for music teachers are expected to grow at an

Musical Instrument Repairers

What Musical Instrument Repairers Do

Musical instrument repairers tune instruments and make other repairs as needed. Most repairers specialize in fixing one type of instrument. Many repairers make regular inspections of pianos, organs, or other instruments to keep them from getting out of tune or developing other problems.

When a piano or other large instrument gets out of tune or develops other problems, repairers make house calls. Repairs range from adjusting a string to the proper pitch to replacing the wooden sounding board that amplifies the sound of the strings. Repairers use screwdrivers, pliers, and other hand tools as well as special restringing tools.

Musical instrument repairers who work on guitars, violins, and other small string instruments play the instrument to listen for particular problems and adjust strings or make other repairs. Repairers may have to take the instrument apart to find a problem or make a repair, using hand tools, such as screwdrivers and pliers, to remove cracked or broken sections. They often use a variety of glues and varnishes.

Wind-instrument repairers work on clarinets, oboes, bassoons, saxophones, and flutes. Common repairs include fixing or replacing the moving parts of the instrument, cutting new padding or corks to replace worn pieces and replacing springs. If the body of the woodwind is cracked in any sections the repairer tries to pin or glue the crack shut. In some situations, the repairer must replace the entire section or joint of the instrument.

Repairing brass instruments such as trumpets and French horns requires skill in metal working and plating. To fix dents, the repairer works the dent out with hammers and more delicate tools and seals splits in the metal with solder. If one of the valves of the brass instrument is leaking, the repairer may replate it and build up layers of metal to fill the gaps.

Percussion tuners and repairers work on drums, bells, congas, timbales, cymbals, and castanets. They may stretch new

EXPLORING

• Take music lessons or classes to develop your musical ear.

• Learn about a variety of instruments. For example, if you play trumpet, you might also experiment with the trombone or French horn. If you play the clarinet, try out a saxophone or an oboe.

• Study physics to learn about the mechanics of sound.

• Shop classes and art classes can teach you woodworking and metalworking skills.

• Hobbies, such as jewelry making and model building, help you learn to handle fine tools and small parts.

cians, but they should be able to play an instrument and know when it is out of tune. Repairers must talk to customers and be able to explain what is wrong with an instrument. Because repairers usually work alone, they must have the discipline to stay with a project until it is finished.

Most repairers learn their skills through on-the-job training. They work in music shops under the supervision of experienced repairers. It takes four to five years of training to become a skilled piano or organ repairer. It takes less time to become qualified in fixing smaller musical instruments. It can take many years to learn how to repair violins and other fine-stringed instruments.

skins over the instrument, replace broken or missing parts, or seal cracks in the wood.

Education and Training

Musical instrument repairers do not have to be expert musi-

Some technical schools offer programs in instrument repair. These programs last from six months to two years. Although they offer some hands-on experience, you would be wise to get additional training with an experienced musical instrument repairer before you start out on your own.

Earnings

Musical instrument repairers and tuners earn from $13,200 to $38,000 a year. The average salary was about $23,000 in 1998. Those in training earn somewhat less, but experienced repairers can earn as much as $49,000 a year, especially if they have a strong reputation for the quality of their work. Earnings are usually higher in urban areas.

Outlook

Although there are millions of instruments in the United States, relatively few people make a living as repairers. This situation is not expected to change through 2008. Jobs are expected to increase more slowly than the average. Most instrument repairers are self-employed and may not have the time to train new workers.

FOR MORE INFO

For information about instrument repair and a list of schools offering courses in the field, contact:
American Guild of Organists
The American Organist Magazine
475 Riverside Drive, Suite 1260
New York, NY 10115
Tel: 212-870-2310
Web: http://www.agohq.org

For information about instrument repair and a list of schools offering courses in the field, contact:
National Association of Professional Band Instrument Repair Technicians
PO Box 51
Normal, IL 61761
Tel: 309-452-4257
Web: http://www.napbirt.org

For information on piano repair, contact the following organization:
Piano Technicians Guild
3930 Washington
Kansas City, MO 64111
Tel: 816-753-7747
Web: http://www.ptg.org

Those with the most training will have the best chance at job opportunities. More repairers and tuners will be needed to work on instruments rented to students, schools, and other organizations.

Musicians

What Musicians Do

Musicians perform, teach, write, arrange, and direct music. Instrumental musicians play one or more musical instruments, usually in a gro up. They play in jazz bands, country and western bands, symphony orchestras, dance bands, pop or rock bands, or other groups.

Classical musicians perform in orchestra concerts, opera and dance performances, and theater orchestras. The most talented may work as soloists with orchestras. Some accompany singers, choirs, and solo musicians on the piano during rehearsals and performances. Classical musicians also perform in churches or accompany church choirs.

Musicians in jazz, blues, country, and pop or rock groups play in bars, nightclubs, festivals, and concert halls. They may perform music for recordings, television, videos, and movie soundtracks. Musicians who play popular music almost always use rhythm instruments, such as piano, bass, drums, and guitar in their groups. They also add melody, harmony, and special effects with all kinds of other acoustic and electronic instruments, such as brass, woodwinds, and synthesizers. Some instruments are unique to one type of music. For example, country and western music often features the slide guitar, banjo, and fiddle. Blues musicians often play harmonica. However, talented musicians can play any type of music on their instruments. Some musicians, especially classical musicians, concentrate on playing one instrument. Others play several instruments, although they often have one instrument that they specialize in.

Many musicians travel a great deal, and few are able to find full-time work. Most have periods of unemployment between jobs and support themselves with other work during the day. Musicians find work all over the country, but most jobs are found in large cities and in areas with large recording industries.

Education and Training

Many colleges and universities have music departments which offer degrees in music, but a music degree is not required for most jobs in instrumental music.

EXPLORING

• Schools and communities give you lots of choices for musical training and performance, including choirs, ensembles, bands, orchestras, musicals, and talent shows.

• If you are taking private lessons, your teacher can arrange for you to give a recital to get performance experience.

• Churches provide opportunities for singers, instrumentalists, and directors to perform and learn.

• Summer music camps give you a chance to perform with others, gain experience on stage, and begin to find out if you have what it takes to become a professional musician.

Courses in music, mathematics, and social science are helpful. Participation in band or choir is useful preparation for a music career. Community groups also offer training and performance in music, dance, singing, and theater, which give you performance experience.

Instrumental musicians begin developing their musical skills at an early age. From then on, long hours of practice and study are necessary. Most musicians train under the supervision of an experienced musician. In addition to learning the technique for an instrument, such as fingering patterns, breathing, embouchure (mouth position for brass and wind players), and tone, musicians also learn music theory, including rhythm, melody, harmony, and notation.

Professional musicians usually belong to an organization called the American Federation of

JAZZ GREAT

ABC Record

Jazz musician John Coltrane (1926-1967) began his professional career performing in bars and clubs in Philadelphia. He played in the bands of Dizzy Gillespie, Thelonious Monk, and Miles Davis. Coltrane made his first album in 1957 and formed his own band in 1960. He played both soprano and tenor saxophone and influenced many musicians with his avant-garde, improvisatory style.

Musicians. Concert soloists also belong to the American Guild of Musical Artists, Inc. These organizations are unions that set standard fees for performances and offer benefits to members, such as health insurance.

Earnings

Earnings for musicians vary greatly, depending on skill, reputation, geographic location, type of music, and number of engagements per year. The type of music that is popular at a given time also affects income.

Musicians in major U.S. symphony orchestras earned salaries of between $21,000 and $95,000 a year during the 1998-99 performance season. The median salary for musicians and singers in 1998 was $30,200. Popular musicians are paid per concert or "gig." Average pay per musician ranges from $30 to $300 per night. Of course, musicians who are well known earn thousands or even millions of dollars each year, but very few musicians achieve such earnings and fame. Studio recording work pays musicians well but is not plentiful. Church organists, choir directors, and soloists earn about $40 to $100 each week, but these positions often are part-time.

Outlook

It is very difficult to earn a living solely as a musician, and competition for jobs during the next decade will continue to be

FOR MORE INFO

The following organizations have information on career opportunities and education resources.

American Federation of Musicians of the United States and Canada
Paramount Building
1501 Broadway, Suite 600
New York, NY 10036
Tel: 212-869-1330
Web: http://www.afm.org

American Guild of Musical Artists
1727 Broadway
New York, NY 10019
Tel: 212-265-3687
Web: http://www.agmanatl.com/

National Association of Schools of Music
11250 Roger Bacon Drive, Suite 21
Reston, VA 20190
Web: http://www.arts-accredit.org/nasm/nasm.htm

as stiff as it has been in the past. Employment of musicians should grow about as fast as the average through 2008. The increase in cable television networks may cause an increase in employment for musicians, as will the growing number of record companies.

Orchestra Conductors

What Orchestra Conductors Do

An orchestra is a group of musicians who play music together. *Orchestra conductors* are the men and women who direct the musicians as they play. Usually, the word orchestra applies to groups larger than six musicians. Smaller groups are called trios, combos, quintets, or bands. Orchestras play many different types of music. Some play jazz, others play dance music, and still others play classical music.

Orchestra conductors have many responsibilities. Their most important task is to decide how a piece of music should be played and then to teach the musicians in the orchestra to play the piece that way. In other words, the conductor helps the orchestra to interpret a piece of music.

In addition to interpreting music, conductors help orchestras to play as a unit. A symphony orchestra, for example, may

An orchestra conductor directs a young people's symphony.

have 50 to 80 musicians who play a variety of instruments. Each group of instruments, such as violins or French horns, has a slightly different musical line to play. Without a strong conductor it would be difficult for all of these musicians to produce a pleasing sound. The conductor sets the beat, decides when the music should be played louder or softer, and indicates which instruments should play at what times.

Conductors work with many different types of orchestras. Some conductors lead symphony orchestras. Others direct orchestras that play during operas, musical plays, or ballet performances. Conductors also lead marching bands, jazz bands, and dance bands.

Education and Training

Conductors should be able to play one or more instruments and must know music

EXPLORING

• Go to as many musical presentations as you can—symphonies, operas, musical theater—and study the conductors. Note their baton techniques and their arm and body movements. Try to determine how the orchestra and audience respond to the gesturing of the conductors.

• There are many reference books and biographies that give detailed information about conductors and their work. Here are some suggestions:

Handbook of Conducting by Herman Scherchen (Oxford University Press, 1990).

The Grammar of Conducting by Max Rudolf (Wadsworth Publishing Company, 1993).

theory, analysis, composition, notation, and sight reading. They need the skills to control the timing, rhythm, and structure of a musical piece. They must command the attention and respect of orchestra members.

There are no formal education requirements for conductors. However, most study music throughout their whole lives. There are conducting programs at some conservatories and universities. Many of the conductor's skills are learned and developed in practice.

Some schools offer courses in music and music appreciation. Other helpful classes include math, dance, and theater. Many schools have student bands and orchestras. However, serious music students usually attend special music schools, called conservatories. Students also study with private teachers.

Earnings

The range of earnings for conductors varies greatly from one category of conductors to another. Many conductors work part-time and have small yearly

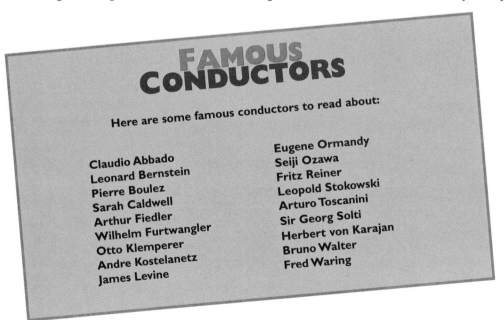

FAMOUS CONDUCTORS

Here are some famous conductors to read about:

Claudio Abbado
Leonard Bernstein
Pierre Boulez
Sarah Caldwell
Arthur Fiedler
Wilhelm Furtwangler
Otto Klemperer
Andre Kostelanetz
James Levine

Eugene Ormandy
Seiji Ozawa
Fritz Reiner
Leopold Stokowski
Arturo Toscanini
Sir Georg Solti
Herbert von Karajan
Bruno Walter
Fred Waring

incomes. Part-time choir directors for churches and synagogues earn $3,500 to $25,000 per year, while full-time directors make from $15,000 to $40,000. Dance band conductors earn $300 to $1,200 per week. Opera and choral group conductors make $8,000 a year working part-time at the community level, but those with permanent positions with established companies in major cities can earn more than $100,000 a year. Symphony orchestra conductors earn $25,000 to $40,000 a year conducting smaller, regional orchestras. The resident conductor of an internationally famous orchestra can earn $500,000 or more a year.

Outlook

The number of orchestras in the United States has grown only slightly in the last two decades. The competition for conductor jobs, already stiff, will become even more stiff in the next decade.

FOR MORE INFO

The following organizations provide information on career and internship opportunities.

American Federation of Musicians of the United States and Canada
1501 Broadway, Suite 600
New York, NY 10036
Tel: 212-869-1330
Web: http://www.afm.org

American Symphony Orchestra League
1156 15th Street, NW, Suite 805
Washington, DC 20005
Tel: 202-776-0212
Email: league@symphony.org
Web: http://www.symphony.org

Conductors' Guild, Inc.
103 South High Street, Room 6
West Chester, PA 19382
Tel: 215-430-6010
Web: http://www.conductorsguild.org/

Association of Canadian Orchestras
56 The Esplanade, Suite 311
Toronto, ON M5E 1A7 Canada
Tel: 416-366-8834
Email: assoc@terraport.net

Pop and Rock Musicians

Readin' About Rock 'n' Roll

The History of Rock and Roll by David Shirley (Franklin Watts, Inc., 1997).

Classic Rock Stories: The Stories Behind the Greatest Songs of All Time by Tim Morse (Griffin Trade Paperback, 1998).

Video Killed the Radio Star: How MTV Rocked the World by Tom McGrath (Random House, 1995).

Pioneers of Rock & Roll: 100 Artists Who Changed the Face of Rock (Watson-Guptill, 1994).

The Ultimate Encyclopedia of Rock, edited by Michael Heatley (Harper Collins, 1993).

What Pop and Rock Musicians Do

Pop and rock musicians perform in clubs, concert halls, on college campuses, and at festivals and fairs. They record their music on CDs and audio cassettes. They often write original music and perform it with other instrumentalists and vocalists.

After writing the music, musicians spend many hours rehearsing the new songs with other band members. Rehearsal and commitment to the band is extremely important to rock musicians. In order for the band to sound as good as it possibly can, all the instrumentalists and vocalists must work together and get to know each other's abilities and styles.

Pop and rock musicians record a demo (demonstration) tape, which they send to club managers and music producers. When making a demo tape, or recording a CD for a record company, they record in a studio and work with recording professionals, such as audio engineers, producers, and mixing engineers. Musicians may also have to audition live for a club manager in addition to providing a demo tape.

When a club books a band, the club's promotional staff may advertise the upcoming performance. Many bands, though, have to attract audiences on their own. They distribute fliers, send press releases to area newspapers, and send out announcements. A popular way to promote a band is to have a Web site listing performance schedules. Advertising for successful groups is usually handled by a record company or promoter.

Very few pop and rock musicians become successful on their recordings alone. Most perform live and gain a following of fans before they make their first recording. For a performance, musicians arrive early to prepare the stage. They set up instruments and sound systems, check sound quality, and become familiar with the stage and facility. The band reviews the list of songs to be performed and it might change the songs based on audience responses.

EXPLORING

• Become involved in your school's various musical groups.

• Try out for school plays and the community theater to get experience performing in front of an audience.

• Attend as many musical performances as possible. They don't all have to be pop and rock concerts. Many clubs and other concert facilities offer shows for all ages, where you can see musical artists perform live.

• Get together with friends or classmates and experiment with playing different musical styles.

• If you are interested in writing pop and rock music, read the lyrics of your favorite songs and try to figure out why you like them. Try to write lyrics and put them to music.

HOW IT ALL BEGAN

The term "rock 'n' roll" was first coined by radio disc jockey Alan Freed in the 1950s. Since then rock music has been an important part of teenage culture. Though much of rock music is popular with all ages now, it was the teen culture that evolved in the 1950s that brought the doo wop and boogie woogie music of the South to audiences all across the country. Teens, for the first time in U.S. history, were spending their own money, and they were spending it on the records they heard on the radio. What had previously been music appreciated primarily by black audiences, was brought to white audiences by the success of Chuck Berry, Little Richard, Fats Domino, and later, Elvis Presley and Jerry Lee Lewis.

Education and Training

It is important to start your music studies as early as possible. You should learn about music theory, the different types of music, how to play one or more instruments, and how to play with other musicians. English composition and creative writing courses will develop your songwriting skills.

A college education isn't necessary for becoming a pop and rock musician, but it can help you learn about music theory

Profile: Chuck Berry

Chuck Berry was an African-American musician with a distinctive guitar style blending blues and country music. He had a knack for writing topical songs relating to teenagers. Berry became one of the most influential performers in the development of rock. Many later performers, especially the Beach Boys, the Beatles, and the Rolling Stones, played his songs and copied his guitar style. He began his recording career in 1955 with "Maybellene." Many other hit records followed, notably "School Day" (1957), "Rock and Roll Music" (1957), "Sweet Little Sixteen" (1958), and "Johnny B. Goode" (1958).

and history. You can pursue an education in audio recording, writing, or music at a community college, university, or trade school. There are a number of seminars, conferences, and workshops available on song-writing, audio recording, and record producing.

Earnings

When starting out, pop and rock musicians are likely to play clubs and events for free. As they gain a following, they may get a percentage of the club's cover charge or drink receipts in exchange for their performance. The most successful pop and rock musicians can make millions of dollars. According to *Forbes Magazine's* "Celebrity 100" ranking of entertainers, the Rolling Stones ranked the highest of any rock group, with an estimated income of $57 million in 1998.

Outlook

There will always be thousands more rock musicians than there are record contracts. But there always will be opportunities for new performers with record companies and clubs. Record companies are always looking for original sounds and talents.

FOR MORE INFO

Contact these organizations to learn about the industry, and opportunities available to young musicians:
American Society of Composers, Authors, and Publishers
One Lincoln Plaza
New York, NY 10023
Tel: 212-621-6000
Web: http://www.ascap.org

National Academy of Songwriters
6255 Sunset Boulevard, Suite 1023
Hollywood, CA 90028
Tel: 800-826-7287

American Federation of Musicians
1501 Broadway, Suite 600
New York, NY 10036
Tel: 212-869-1330
Web: http://www.afm.org

RELATED JOBS

Audio Recording Engineers
Composers
Music Producers
Musical Directors and Conductors
Musicians
Singers
Songwriters

Screenwriters

What Screenwriters Do

Screenwriters write scripts for motion pictures or television. The themes may be their own ideas or stories assigned by a producer or director. Often, screenwriters are hired to turn popular plays or novels into screenplays. Writers of original screenplays create their own stories which are produced for the motion picture industry or television. Screenwriters may also write television programs, such as comedies, dramas, documentaries, variety shows, and entertainment specials.

Screenwriters must not only be creative, but they must also have excellent research skills. For projects such as historical movies, documentaries, and medical or science programs, research is a very important step.

Screenwriters start with an outline, or a treatment, of the story's plot. When the director or producer approves the story outline, screenwriters then complete the story for production. During the writing process, screenwriters write many drafts of the script. They frequently meet with directors and producers to discuss script changes.

Some screenwriters work alone and others work on teams with other writers. Many specialize in certain types of scripts, such as drama, comedy, documentaries, motion pictures, or television. Motion picture screenwriters usually write alone and exclusively for movies. Screenwriters for television series work very long hours in the studio. Many television shows have limited runs, so much of the work for television screenwriters is not continuous.

Education and Training

In high school, you should develop your writing skills in English, theater, speech, and journalism classes. Social studies and foreign language can also be helpful in creating intelligent scripts.

One important quality a screenwriter must have is a creative imagination and the ability to tell a story. The best way to prepare for a career as a screenwriter is to write and read every day. A college

EXPLORING

• One of the best ways to learn about screenwriting is to read and study scripts. Watch a motion picture while following the script at the same time.

• Read film-industry publications, such as *Daily Variety, Hollywood Reporter,* and *The Hollywood Scriptwriter.*

• There are a number of books that teach you the format for a screenplay. There are also computer software programs that help with screenplay formatting.

• Write a play for your classmates or friends to perform. Have a friend who is interested in film videotape the performance.

WOMEN SCREENWRITERS MAKE HISTORY

Women screenwriters were much more prominent in the early days of filmmaking. One-half of the films made before 1925 were written by women, such as Frances Marion (*Stella Dallas*, *The Scarlet Letter*) and Anita Loos (*The Women*). Marion was the highest paid screenwriter from 1916 to the 1930s, and she served as the first vice president of the Writer's Guild. Though a smaller percentage of feature films written by women are produced today, more women screenwriters have won Academy Awards since 1985 than in all the previous years. Among recent Oscar winners are Ruth Prawer Jhabvala for *Howard's End* and Emma Thompson for *Sense and Sensibility*.

degree is not required, but a liberal arts education is helpful because it exposes you to a wide range of subjects. While in school, become involved in theater to learn about all of the elements required by a screenplay, such as characters, plots, and themes. Book clubs, creative writing classes, and film study are also good ways to learn the basic elements of screenwriting.

Earnings

Annual wages for screenwriters vary widely. Some screenwriters make hundreds of thousands of dollars from their scripts. Others write and film their own scripts without any payment at all, relying on backers and loans. Screenwriters who work independently do not earn regular salaries. They are paid a fee for each script they write. Those who write for ongoing television shows do earn regular salaries. According to the Writers Guild of America (WGA), the median income for WGA members is $83,542 a year.

Outlook

The job market for screenwriters, especially in film and television, is highly competitive because so many people are attracted to the field. In this industry, it is helpful to network and make contacts. In motion picture screenwriting, and in the creation of new television shows, persistence is important. On the brighter side, the growth of the cable industry has increased demand for original screenplays and adaptations.

If you are thinking about a screenwriting career, you should also be open to careers in technical writing, journalism, or copywriting. Academic

FOR MORE INFO

To learn more about the film industry, to read interviews and articles by noted screenwriters, and to find links to many other screenwriting-related sites on the Internet, visit the WGA Web site:

Writers Guild of America (WGA)
West Chapter
7000 West Third Street
Los Angeles, CA 90048
Tel: 310-550-1000
Web: http://www.wga.org

Writers Guild of America, East Chapter
555 West 57th Street
New York, NY 10019
Tel: 212-767-7800
Web: http://www.wgaeast.org

preparation in a related field may help you find another occupation in case a screenwriting job does not happen right away.

RELATED JOBS

Public Relations Specialists
Songwriters
Writers

Singers

What Singers Do

Singers, or *vocalists,* are musicians whose instruments are their voices. They use their knowledge of musical tone, phrasing, harmony, and melody to create vocal music.

Singers are classified in two ways. The first way is by the range of their voices. Sopranos have the highest voices, followed by mezzo-sopranos, contraltos (or altos), tenors, baritones, and basses, who have the lowest voices. The second way that singers may be classified is by the type of music they sing, such as classical, rock, folk, opera, jazz, or country.

Nearly all singers work with instrumental musicians. A singer's backup group may be as small as one piano player or a single guitarist or as large as a full symphony orchestra. In between are jazz combos, dance bands, and rock bands. Singers also work in choirs, barbershop quartets, and other singing groups, with or without accompaniment.

Profile: Marian Anderson

The resonant low tones and natural beauty of Marian Anderson's (1897-1993) contralto voice made her famous as a singer of spirituals, lieder (German art songs), and arias. She became the first African-American singer to join the Metropolitan Opera Company. She made her debut as Ulrica in *A Masked Ball* in 1955.

In 1939 Anderson received national attention when the Daughters of the American Revolution refused to let her sing in Constitution Hall in Washington, DC, because of her race. Eleanor Roosevelt and others organized a concert at the Lincoln Memorial and on Easter Sunday morning she sang before an audience of 75,000. In the same year, Anderson received the Spingarn Medal for outstanding achievement by a Black American. She retired from the concert stage in 1965.

Her autobiography is *My Lord, What a Morning* (1956).

Kranner Center for the Performing Arts

A singer performs on stage in an operetta.

EXPLORING

• Join music clubs at school and sing in choirs or ensembles.
• Many singers get their start singing in their church at an early age.
• Take part in school drama productions that involve musical numbers.
• Audition for roles in community musical productions.
• There are many summer programs offered throughout the United States for students interested in singing and other performing arts. For example, Stanford University offers its Stanford Jazz Workshop each summer for students who are at least 12 years old. It offers activities in instrumental and vocal music, as well as swimming and other sports. For more information, contact the university at Box 11291, Stanford, CA 94309.

Many singers travel throughout the country and even the world to perform live for audiences. Some singers, especially those who sing classical music, sing in more than one language. Operas, for example, are often written in Italian, French, and German, so singers must be able to pronounce and understand the lyrics. Some singers are primarily studio singers. That is, they rarely perform in front of audiences but instead record their singing in sound studios. They may record television and radio commercials, or perform songs for CDs and tape recordings.

Singers can also be actors. Musical plays on the stage require singers with strong voices who can also act well. Actors who can sing will find more job opportunities in the theater if they can dance as well.

Education and Training

Most singers begin learning their skills at an early age. Young children can sing in school or church choirs. Students can join concert choirs or take part in musical plays.

Most professional singers have singing teachers and voice coaches. They practice vocal exercises every day, such as scales and intervals, breath control, and diction exercises to increase the range, power, and clarity of their voices. Some colleges and universities offer music degrees with a concentration in voice.

HIGH TO LOW: WHAT'S YOUR RANGE?

Soprano: The highest female voice. Its normal range is from middle C to A, but trained sopranos range from B flat to high C. A *coloratura soprano* has a light, soaring voice that can reach notes as high as F, sometimes even to C above high C. A *lyric soprano* combines a rich tone with the agility of a coloratura. A *dramatic soprano* has a rich, intense, emotional voice slightly lower than a coloratura.

Mezzo-soprano: A middle voice between the soprano and the contralto. Normal range, about two octaves, is from B to G.

Contralto, or Alto: The lowest female voice. It has a heavy, rich quality, with a normal range from G to E.

Tenor: The highest natural male voice. Normal range is from E to A. (Falsetto is a higher but unnatural pitch. A *dramatic tenor* has a full, powerful voice, with a range from C to B flat or C. Lyric tenors have a lighter quality and sing notes as high as C sharp above middle C.

Baritone: A middle voice between bass and tenor. The typical range is from G to F.

Bass: The lowest and deepest male voice. The usual range is from E to D. A trained bass can go as low as C two octaves below middle C and as high as F above middle C.

Earnings

Singing is often considered a glamorous occupation. However, competition for positions is very high. Only a small number of those who want to be singers find glamorous jobs and earn high salaries.

Starting salaries can be as low as $6,900 per year or even less. Average salaries are around $26,000. The top earners in studio and opera earn an average of $70,000 per year, although some earn much more. Singers in an opera chorus earn between $600 and $800 per week. Classical soloists receive between $2,000 and $3,000 for each performance, while choristers receive around $70 per performance. Many singers supplement their earnings by working at other positions, such as teaching at schools or giving private lessons.

Outlook

There always has been strong competition for the limited number of job opportunities for

FOR MORE INFO

For more information about a career as a singer, contact the following:

American Federation of Musicians of the United States and Canada
Paramount Building
1501 Broadway, Suite 600
New York, NY 10036

American Guild of Musical Artists
1727 Broadway
New York, NY 10019
Web: http://www.agmanatl.com/

**Musicians National
Hot Line Association**
277 East 6100 South
Salt Lake City, UT 84107

singers. Usually only the most talented will find regular employment. Because most singers only find part-time job opportunities, it is best for aspiring singers to also consider music-related jobs that will provide a steady income. Employment in composition, education, broadcasting, therapy, or community arts management is far more secure.

Songwriters

What Songwriters Do

Songwriters write the words and sometimes the music for songs, including songs for recordings, advertising jingles, and theatrical performances. They may also perform these songs. Songwriters who write only the words and not the music are called *lyricists*.

Songwriters may choose to write about emotions, such as love or sadness. They put their ideas into a small number of words, focusing on the sounds of the words together. Many songwriters carry a notebook and write about things that they hear or see. They may write songs about people, events, or experiences. They may write about broad themes that will be understood by everyone, getting ideas from current events or social situations such as poverty, racial issues, or war. Or they may write about personal issues, based on their own experiences or conversations with others.

Songwriters usually have a musical style in mind when they write lyrics. These styles include pop, rock, hip hop, rap, country, blues, jazz, and classical.

Songwriters who work for advertising agencies have to write about certain products for radio and television commercials. Producers also hire songwriters to write lyrics for opera, Broadway shows, or movies.

Many songwriters have a certain method for writing songs. Sometimes, they write the title first because it allows them to capture a theme in just a few words. The first words of the song are often the strongest, to get the attention of the listener. Many songwriters find that there are about four common characteristics found in a song: an identifiable, universal idea; a memorable title; a strong beginning; and an appropriate form, including rhythm, verse, and refrain.

Lyricists who do not write music work with a composer. The composer might play a few measures on an instrument and the lyricist tries to write words that fit well with the music. Or, the lyricist suggests a few words or lines and the composer tries to write music that fits the

EXPLORING

• Learn to play a musical instrument, especially the piano or guitar. Start writing your own songs.

• Join a rock group to gain experience writing music for several musicians.

• Most schools and communities have orchestras, bands, and choruses that are open to performers.

• Work on a student-written musical show.

There are a number of books available to help you start writing songs. Here are a few:

• *The Songwriter's Idea Book: 40 Strategies to Excite Your Imagination, Help You Design Distinctive Songs, and Keep Your Creative Flow* by Sheila Davis (Writers Digest Books, 1996).

• *How to Make a Good Song a Hit Song: Rewriting and Marketing Your Lyrics and Music* by Molly-Ann Leikin (Hal Leonard Publishing, 1996).

• *Beginning Songwriters Answer Book* by Paul Zollo (Writer's Digest Books, 1993).

• *Writing Better Lyrics* by Pat Pattison (Writers Digest Books, 1995).

88 Songwriting Wrongs & How to Right Them by Pat Luboff and Pete Luboff (Writers Digest Books).

Kids Can Write Songs Too by Frank E. Cooke (Frank E. Cooke, 1986).

words. Each partner must trust the other's talent and be able to cooperate to work out a full song.

Education and Training

Songwriters must have a good understanding of language and grammar. In high school, you should take courses in English composition, poetry, music theory, and journalism. Learning how to play a musical instrument is a good idea. You also should take classes in musical composition.

There is really no formal training that a songwriter must have in order to write songs. Musical training is important, though. Songwriting workshops often are offered by community colleges and music schools. College music programs teach you how to read music and understand harmony. They also expose you to a variety of musical styles.

Earnings

Songwriters' earnings vary from almost nothing to many millions of dollars. A songwriter may write songs for several years before actually selling or recording a song. Royalties from a song may reach $20,000 per year or more for each song. A successful songwriter may earn $100,000 or more a year from the royalties of several songs.

Outlook

Songwriters find much competition in their field. It is a career much like acting, in which many people are attracted to the work. But to be a successful songwriter requires much hard work. It takes many submissions of songs to earn a reputation and become successful. Songwriters should find more opportunities outside of the recording industry, writing music for original cable programming, multimedia projects, advertising, and the Internet.

FOR MORE INFO

Contact these organizations to learn about the industry, and opportunities available to young songwriters and musicians:

American Society of Composers, Authors, and Publishers
One Lincoln Plaza
New York, NY 10023
Tel: 212-621-6000
Web: http://www.ascap.org

Broadcast Music, Inc.
320 West 57th Street
New York, NY 10019-3790
Tel: 212-586-2000
Web: http://www.bmi.com

National Academy of Songwriters
6255 Sunset Boulevard, Suite 1023
Hollywood, CA 90028
Tel: 800-826-7287
Email: nassong@aol.com
Web: http://www.nassong.org

RELATED JOBS

Composers
Lyricists
Poets
Writers

Stage Production Technicians

Let There Be Light

Lighting equipment and operation is one of the more complex parts of stage production. Here are some lighting terms to know:

Fader: Controls the output level of a lantern (lamp)

Floodlights: Lights that give a general, fixed spread of light

Follow spot: Light directed at actor that can follow all movements

Footlights: Lights set into the stage floor that throw strong general light into the performers' faces

Gel: Colored medium inserted in front of the light to change the color of a beam

Ghost: A beam of light that leaks from a light and falls where it is not wanted

Gobo: A screen placed in front of a stage light to cast a particular image on stage; also a cut-out shape that is projected

Iris: A device within a lantern that allows a technician to change the size of a circular beam

What Stage Production Technicians Do

Stage production technicians install lights, sound equipment, and scenery for theater stages. They build the stages for theatrical and musical events in parks, stadiums, and other places. For small productions, stage workers must be able to do a variety of tasks, while for larger productions, such as those on Broadway, stage technicians may be responsible for only one or two tasks. Stage production technicians can be carpenters, prop makers, lighting designers, lighting-equipment operators, sound technicians, electricians, and riggers.

Stage technicians use diagrams of the stage and written instructions from the stage designer. They talk to the stage manager to decide what kinds of sets, scenery, props, lighting, and sound equipment are required. Then they collect or build the props or scenery, using hammers, saws, and other hand and power

Stage production technicians move heavy scenery between acts of a play.

lighting and sound equipment.

Education and Training

Stage production technicians must be high school graduates. Many employers prefer to hire stage technicians who are graduates of two-year junior or community colleges. If you are interested in stage production work you should make sure to take courses in math,

tools. Stage technicians position lights and sound equipment on or around the stage. They clamp light fixtures to supports and connect electrical wiring from the fixtures to power sources and control panels. During rehearsals and performances, stage technicians pull ropes and cables that raise and lower curtains and other equipment. Sometimes they also operate the

EXPLORING

• Participate in school theatrical performances. Try out acting, stage design, costume design, prop making, lighting, and special effects.

• Volunteer to do behind-the-scenes work for amateur community theater productions or special benefit events.

English, drama, and history. Carpentry or electronics courses that include work with lighting and sound will be helpful. Participate in the various parts of school theatrical performances, from acting to working on sets to helping with promotion.

Earnings

Most stage technicians earn between $20,000 and $30,000 a year. Salaries depend on the employer, geographic location, and the technician's responsibilities.

THEATER WORDS TO KNOW

Apron: A slight extension of the stage beyond the proscenium arch

Arena stage: A stage in the center of the auditorium, surrounded by the audience

Backdrop: A painted canvas curtain across the back of the stage

Flat: A covered panel, usually of painted canvas, used as scenery

Flies: An area above the stage where scenery may be hung for storage

Properties, or **props:** Furnishings and accessories used onstage

Proscenium, or **picture-frame, stage:** A stage that is recessed into the stagehouse. The audience views the performance through the proscenium arch, a frame around the stage. The stage can be closed off with a curtain.

Revolving stage: An immense turntable in the floor of the stagehouse, generally as wide as, or wider than, the proscenium opening, upon which two or three sets may be built. Revolving the turntable brings a new set into view.

Set: The scenery and furnishings for a scene

Stage wagon: A rolling platform on which scenery or even a whole set may be built and which is moved onstage for the scene

Teaser: A flat or curtain running across the top of the proscenium opening

Thrust stage: A stage that extends into the auditorium

Tormentors: Flats or curtains at the sides of the proscenium opening, which with the teaser form an inner frame of the proscenium arch

Stage technicians who are hired for their skills as carpenters, electricians, or sound or light technicians earn salaries roughly equal to the salaries they would receive elsewhere, which range from $14,000 to $30,000 a year. Carpenters are generally at the low end and electricians are at the high end. According to Theater Communications Group, scene shop supervisors earn about $27,000 a year and stage managers earn about $31,000 a year.

Outlook

If the economy remains strong, employment opportunities for stage production technicians should be good. According to Theatre Communications Group, the industry is remaining steady. There are few new theaters that can afford to pay living wages for stage production workers and technicians, but older and well-established theaters are healthy and surviving. People who can do a variety of tasks stand the best chance of employment.

FOR MORE INFO

This labor union represents technicians, artisans, and craftspersons in the entertainment industry, including live theater, film, and television production.
International Alliance of Theatrical Stage Employees
1515 Broadway, Suite 601
New York, NY 10036
Tel: 212-730-1770
Web: http://www.iatse.lm.com

This organization has information on educational programs, surveys, and publications.
Theater Communications Group
355 Lexington Avenue, 4th Floor
New York, NY 10017
Tel: 212-697-5230
Web: http://www.tcg.org/

RELATED JOBS

Audio Recording Engineers
Carpenters
Construction Laborers
Costume Designers
Electricians
Film and Television Directors
Lighting Technicians
Producers
Special Effects Technicians

Stunt Performers

Stunt Specialties

Here are some of the skills stunt performers learn in training programs at The United Stuntmen's Association (See *For More Info*):

Precision driving

Weaponry

Unarmed combat

Horse work

Fire burns

Stair falls

Climbing and rapelling

Martial arts

High falls

What Stunt Performers Do

Stunt performers work on film scenes that are risky and dangerous. They act out car crashes and chases, fist and sword fights, and falls from cars, motorcycles, horses, and buildings. They perform airplane and helicopter gags, ride through river rapids, and face wild animals. Some stunt performers specialize in one type of stunt.

There are two general types of stunt roles: *double* and *nondescript*. The first requires a stunt performer to double, or take the place of, a star actor in a dangerous scene. As a double, the stunt performer must portray the character in the same way as the star actor. In a nondescript role, the stunt performer does not stand in for another actor, but plays an incidental character in a dangerous scene. An example of a nondescript role is a driver in a freeway chase scene. Stunt performers rarely have speaking parts.

The idea for a stunt usually begins with the screenwriter. Once the stunts are written into the script, it is the job of the director to decide how they will appear on the screen. Directors, especially of large, action-filled movies, often seek the help of a *stunt coordinator.* A stunt coordinator can quickly determine if a stunt is possible and what is the best and safest way to perform it. The stunt coordinator plans the stunt, oversees the setup and construction of special sets and materials, and either hires or recommends the most qualified stunt performer.

Although a stunt may last only a few seconds on film, preparations for the stunt can take several hours or even days. Stunt performers work with props, makeup, wardrobe, and set design departments. They also work closely with the special effects team. A carefully planned stunt can often be completed in just one take. It is more common for the stunt person to perform the stunt several times until the director is satisfied with the performance.

Stunt performers take great care to ensure their safety. They use air bags, body pads, or cables in stunts involving falls or crashes. If a stunt performer must enter a

EXPLORING

• Stunt performers must be in top physical shape and train like athletes. To develop your physical strength and coordination, play on community sports teams and participate in school athletics.

• Acting in school or church plays can teach you about taking direction.

• Theme parks and circuses use stunt performers. Some of these places allow you to meet the performers after shows.

FAMOUS DAREDEVILS

Stunt performers have been around much longer than the film industry. Throughout the 19th century, circus performers leaped from buildings, hung from their necks, walked tight-ropes, swallowed swords, and stuffed themselves into tiny boxes.

Harry Houdini is one of the most famous showmen in entertainment history. Another daredevil was **Samuel Gilbert Scott** who showed "extraordinary and surpassing powers in the art of leaping and diving." After swinging about a ship's riggings or jumping from a 240-foot cliff, he'd pass around a hat for contributions. His final stunt took place at Waterloo Bridge. While performing predive acrobatics with a rope around his neck, he slipped and strangled to death.

burning building, he or she wears special fire-proof clothing and protective cream on the skin.

Education and Training

No standard training exists for stunt performers. They usually start out by contacting stunt coordinators and asking for work. If the stunt coordinator thinks the person has the proper credentials, he or she will be hired for basic stunt work like fight scenes. There are a number of stunt schools, such as the United Stuntmen's Association National Stunt Training School.

Not for Men Only

Women daredevils in the 19th century drew as many spectators as the men. **Signora Josephine Girardelli** was known as the "Fire-Proof Lady." She earned that title by holding boiling oil in her mouth and hands and performing other feats of stamina. **Bess Houdini** assisted her husband Harry in many famous tricks, including one which ended with her tied up and sealed in a trunk. **May Wirth** was a talented equestrian, known as "The Wonder Rider of the World" for her somersaults and other stunts while riding a rushing horse. Even amateurs got into the act—**Annie Taylor,** a 63-year-old Michigan schoolteacher, became the first person to go over the Niagara Falls in a barrel.

Stunt performers get a lot of training on the job. Every new type of stunt has its own problems. By working closely with stunt coordinators, you learn how to eliminate most of the risks involved in stunts. Even so, injuries are very common among stunt performers, and there is even the possibility of death in very dangerous stunts.

Earnings

Stunt performers receive the same day rate as other actors, plus extra pay for more difficult and dangerous stunts. Stunt performers must belong to the actor's union, the Screen Actor's Guild (SAG). The SAG minimum day rate is around $550. A stunt coordinator earns a daily minimum wage of $950, and a weekly minimum of $3,750.

Outlook

There are over 2,500 stunt performers who belong to SAG, but only a small number work on films full-time. It is difficult for new stunt performers to break

FOR MORE INFO

Visit the SAG Web site to read the online stunt performer's guide:
Screen Actor's Guild
5757 Wilshire Boulevard
Los Angeles, CA 90036
Web: http://www.sag.com

For information about the USA training program, contact:
United Stuntmen's Association
2723 Saratoga Lane
Everett, WA 98203
Web: http://www.stuntschool.com

into the business. The future of the profession may be affected by computer technology. Filmmakers today use special effects and computer-generated imagery for action sequences. Computers are also safer. Safety on film sets has always been a serious concern since many stunts are very dangerous. However, using live stunt performers can give a scene more authenticity, so talented stunt performers will always be in demand.

Glossary

accredited: Approved as meeting established standards for providing good training and education. This approval is usually given by an independent organization of professionals to a school or a program in a school. Compare **certified** and **licensed**.

apprentice: A person who is learning a trade by working under the supervision of a skilled worker. Apprentices often receive classroom instruction in addition to their supervised practical experience.

apprenticeship: 1. A program for training apprentices (see apprentice). 2. The period of time when a person is an apprentice. In highly skilled trades, apprenticeships may last three or four years.

associate's degree: An academic rank or title granted by a community or junior college or similar institution to graduates of a two-year program of education beyond high school.

bachelor's degree: An academic rank or title given to a person who has completed a four-year program of study at a college or university. Also called an undergraduate degree or baccalaureate.

certified: Approved as meeting established requirements for skill, knowledge, and experience in a particular field. People are certified by the organization of professionals in their field. Compare **accredited** and **licensed**.

community college: A public two-year college, attended by students who do not live at the college. Graduates of a community college receive an associate degree and may transfer to a four-year college or university to complete a bachelor's degree. Compare **junior college** and **technical college**.

diploma: A certificate or document given by a school to show that a person has completed a course or has graduated from the school.

doctorate: An academic rank or title (the highest) granted by a graduate school to a person who has completed a two- to three-year program after having received a master's degree.

fringe benefit: A payment or benefit to an employee in addition to regular wages or salary. Examples of fringe benefits include a pension, a paid vacation, and health or life insurance.

graduate school: A school that people may attend after they have received their bachelor's degree. People who complete an educational program at a graduate school earn a master's degree or a doctorate.

intern: An advanced student (usually one with at least some college training) in a professional field who is employed in a job that is intended to provide supervised practical experience for the student.

internship: 1. The position or job of an intern (see intern). 2. The period of time when a person is an intern.

junior college: A two-year college that offers courses like those in the first half of a four-year college program. Graduates of a junior college usually receive an associate degree and may transfer to a four-year college or university to complete a bachelor's degree. Compare **community college.**

liberal arts: The subjects covered by college courses that develop broad general knowledge rather than specific occupational skills. The liberal arts are often considered to include philosophy, literature and the arts, history, language, and some courses in the social sciences and natural sciences.

licensed: Having formal permission from the proper authority to carry out an activity that would be illegal without that permission. For example, a person may be licensed to practice medicine or to drive a car. Compare **certified**.

major: (in college) The academic field in which a student specializes and receives a degree.

master's degree: An academic rank or title granted by a graduate school to a person who has completed a one- or two-year program after having received a bachelor's degree.

pension: An amount of money paid regularly by an employer to a former employee after he or she retires from working.

private: 1. Not owned or controlled by the government (such as private industry or a private employment agency). 2. Intended only for a particular person or group; not open to all (such as a private road or a private club).

public: 1. Provided or operated by the government (such as a public library). 2. Open and available to everyone (such as a public meeting).

regulatory: Having to do with the rules and laws for carrying out an activity. A regulatory agency, for example, is a government organization that sets up required procedures for how certain things should be done.

scholarship: A gift of money to a student to help the student pay for further education.

social studies: Courses of study (such as civics, geography, and history) that deal with how human societies work.

starting salary: Salary paid to a newly hired employee. The starting salary is usually a smaller amount than is paid to a more experienced worker.

technical college: A private or public college offering two- or four-year programs in technical subjects. Technical colleges offer courses in both general and technical subjects and award associate degrees and bachelor's degrees.

technician: A worker with specialized practical training in a mechanical or scientific subject who works under the supervision of scientists, engineers, or other professionals. Technicians typically receive two years of college-level education after high school.

technologist: A worker in a mechanical or scientific field with more training than a technician. Technologists typically must have between two and four years of college-level education after high school.

undergraduate: A student at a college or university who has not yet received a degree.

undergraduate degree: See **bachelor's degree**.

union: An organization whose members are workers in a particular industry or company. The union works to gain better wages, benefits, and working conditions for its members. Also called a labor union or trade union.

vocational school: A public or private school that offers training in one or more skills or trades. Compare **technical college**.

wage: Money that is paid in return for work done, especially money paid on the basis of the number of hours or days worked.

Index of Job Titles

Performing Arts on the Web

About.com Language Arts for Kids: Drama and Theater
http:/'kidslangarts.about.com/kids/kidslangarts/msubdrama.htm

ABT's Ballet Dictionary
http://www.abt.org/dictionary

Acting Workshop On-Line
http://www.execpc.com/~blankda/acting2.html

Actingbiz
http://actingbiz.com

And They Kept on Dancing
http://library.thinkquest.org/JO02266F/

CBC4Kids—Music
http://www.cbc4kids.ca/general/music/

Children's Creative Theater Guide
http://tqjunior.thinkquest.org/5291/

Music Notes
http://library.thinkquest.org/15413/

Pop Music Jobs
http://www.pop-music.net/index.asp?pg=popworld/
gonnabe/jobs/jobs.asp

Studio to Stage
http://library.thinkquest.org/21702/